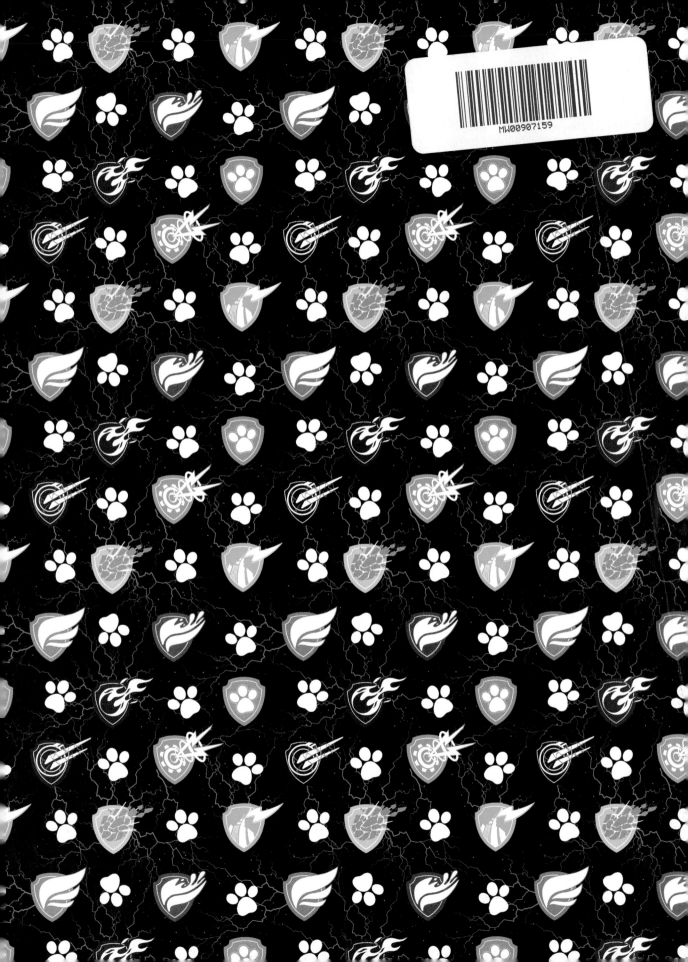

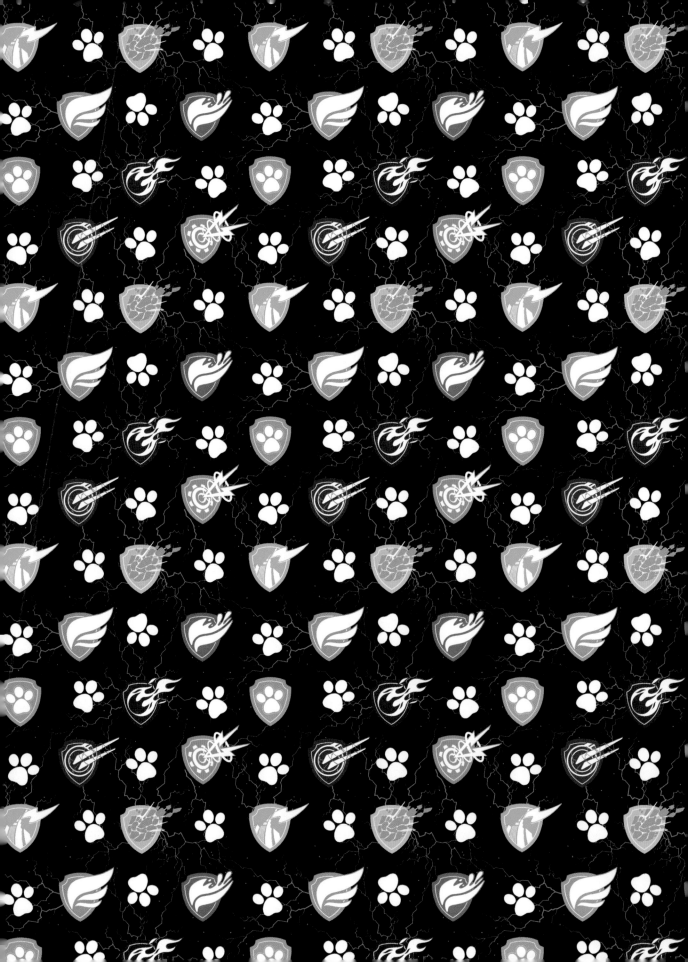

THE OFFICIAL STORYBOOK

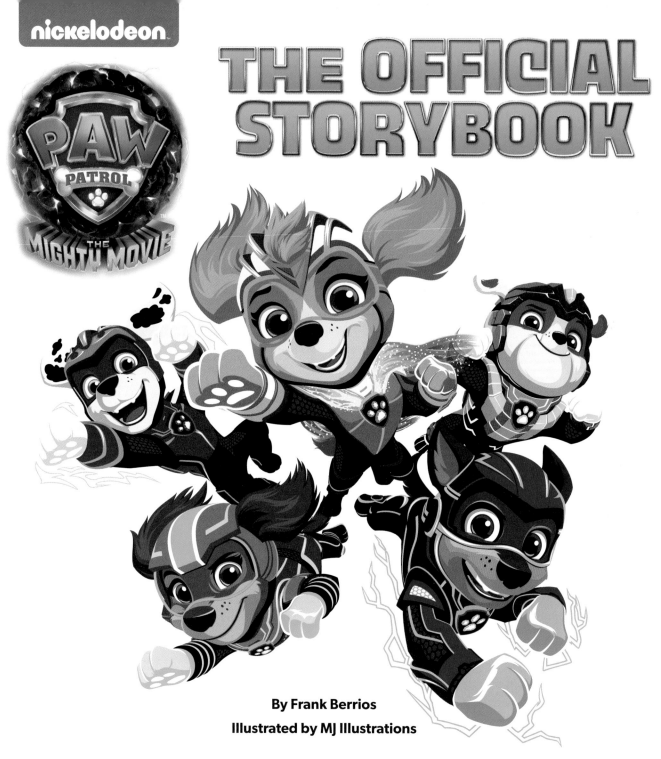

By Frank Berrios

Illustrated by MJ Illustrations

Random House 🏠 New York

rhcbooks.com

ISBN 978-0-593-30419-8 (trade)

Printed in the United States of America

10 9 8 7 6 5 4 3 2

It was another busy day in Adventure City for Ryder and the PAW Patrol—they had just finished fighting a fire at a junkyard.

"Oh, thank you! Thank you!" said the owners, Janet and Hank.

"We're just glad there's not too much damage," said Ryder.

While the pups cleaned up, Chase learned that someone had stolen a giant electromagnet from the scrapyard.

"Who would want to steal a ten-ton electromagnet?" asked Ryder.

Later, everyone in Adventure City prepared to watch a meteor shower—except Victoria Vance, also known as Vee. She had plans for the electromagnet she had stolen from the junkyard.

"My latest invention, the Meteor Magnet, will grab one of those meteors and gently deliver it to my doorstep," said Vee, recording an internet video. "When I catch it, I'm going to be the most famous scientist in the world!"

Back at the Pup Tower, Ryder introduced the team to the Junior Patrollers: Nano, Mini, and Tot. "They're working on their astronomy merit badges, so I invited them to watch the meteor shower with us," he said.

"I don't know about this whole Junior Patrollers thing," grumbled Liberty. "When did the PAW Patrol become a babysitting service?"

"Don't write them off just because they're small," replied Skye.

Little did the pups know, they were in danger—Vee had lost control of the meteor she was trying to catch. Now it was headed straight for Adventure City!

"Everybody out of the street!" yelled Chase. "You need to take cover now!"

"Take shelter!" shouted Ryder as the meteor smashed into the tower, ripped through the street, and landed on the ground as a meterorite. When the dust settled and the pups saw what the meteorite had done, they couldn't believe their home and vehicles were gone!

"The meteorite is giving off some kind of strange energy pulse," said Ryder. "Let's get it out of here until we find what's going on."

Because of her internet video, everyone knew that Vee had caused the crash. She was quickly arrested and put in the Adventure City Jail, where she soon made a new friend.

"Hello, roomie," said the former mayor of Adventure City—and the PAW Patrol's archrival.

It was Mayor Humdinger!

Luckily, Ryder had a new aircraft carrier that he and the pups could stay on. While they were there, he ran tests on the mysterious space rock.

"This will analyze the meteorite and tell us what it's made of," Ryder said. "We'll leave it to scan overnight and see what we can learn tomorrow."

Later that night, while the pups were sleeping, Skye was awakened by a strange noise—it was coming from the meteorite!

Skye went to the lab and touched the meteorite lightly with her paw. She was surprised when it fell apart!

"I didn't do it," she said aloud. Then the crystal core of the meteorite split into seven shards.

When Skye took hold of one of the glowing shards, something strange happened—she began to float! The crystal attached itself to her collar, and suddenly, she could fly! She was also super strong!

"Looks like the smallest pup just became the strongest pup!" chuckled Skye as she tested her new powers.

The other pups and Ryder woke up after Skye accidentally punched through a metal wall!

"What's going on? Is everybody okay?" asked Ryder as Skye floated in the middle of the room.

"I think I've got . . . superpowers!" replied Skye.

"This is the weirdest dream I've ever had," said Rubble.

One by one, the pups approached the crystal pieces, which attached themselves to their collars. Instantly, all the pups had superpowers!

"Whoa!" said Marshall as he created a fireball with his paw.

"Well, that makes sense," replied Chase. "You're a fire pup!"

Chase soon learned that he had super speed, while Zuma could transform into water! Rocky was a walking magnet, and Rubble could become a wrecking ball. But nothing seemed to happen to Liberty. She didn't seem to have a superpower.

"What a rip-off!" she said. "Skye can fly. Marshall can control fire. Zuma turns to water—it's like these crystals amplify something about you."

"Now that we're super, we're going to need a new name for ourselves," said Rubble.
"How about the Mighty Pups?" suggested Ryder.
The pups loved it!

The Mighty Pups even made the news!

"We used to think of big-budget Hollywood movies when we heard the word 'superheroes,'" said Sam Stringer. "But now we know that superheroes are real. They've arrived in Adventure City, and they call themselves the Mighty Pups!"

"They've got new powers, new uniforms, and new merchandise," continued Stringer. "Thanks to the superpowers contained in that mysterious meteorite, the Mighty Pups are truly unstoppable!"

Vee watched the newscast from jail.

"That was my meteorite! Those should be *my* superpowers," she cried. "As soon as I find a way out of here, I'm going to get my meteorite back!"

"We'll help you get out of here if you promise to share some of those superpowers with me," said Humdinger. "Do we have a deal?"

"It's a deal," said Vee.

Humdinger revealed his escape tunnel, which ran down through a toilet. Yuck! But in they went, and before long, they were free!

"Ah, the sweet smell of freedom," said Humdinger.

Back on the aircraft carrier, Liberty decided to train the new recruits.

"Are you three puffballs serious about joining the PAW Patrol?" she asked. They answered affirmatively. "Then I'm going to teach you everything I know and turn you into lean, mean, fluffy little rescue machines!"

Meanwhile, Vee had a plan to use Humdinger's jet to get the superpowers from the PAW Patrol. As soon as she and the former mayor, along with his kittens, were up in the air, she opened an emergency exit and tossed a snack cart into one of the jet's engines.

"Now we'll just fly around until the PAW Patrol comes to rescue us," she said.

Ryder was watching the Junior Patrollers train when his PupPad began to ring.

"PAW Patrol here—what's your emergency?" he asked.

"Mayday, mayday!" yelled Vee. "This is flight HD9904, and we need immediate assistance!"

"Hang tight—we're on our way!" replied Ryder.

"Skye, I need you to fly up there and carry that plane down safely. Are you up for it?"

"I'm a Mighty Pup. I was made for this!" said Skye.

"We'll provide ground support!" said Ryder. "Come on, pups!"

With her superpowers, Skye quickly caught up to the damaged jet. But when Vee stole her collar, she realized it was a trick!

"It's like taking candy from a baby," said Vee, before jumping out of the plane. Humdinger and his kitties quickly followed.

"Thank you for flying Air Humdinger!" he said.

"Ryder, come in—this is Skye," she said. "It was a trap! They stole my crystal! I've got no powers, and this plane is going down!"

"Skye, we're clearing a runway. Set a course for Main Street," replied Ryder.

The pups wasted no time. Marshall handled crowd control while Rubble patched up a hole in the street. Then Chase marked the runway with flares.

Skye was able to land safely, but she was upset about losing her crystal.

"When I had my superpowers, for the first time in my life, I didn't feel like the smallest and the weakest," she told Chase. "I'd do anything to get that crystal back."

Meanwhile, Ryder had bad news for Liberty, Nano, Mini, and Tot.

"We've got to end the Junior Patrollers program," he said. "It's too dangerous. Hopefully we can start it again when things are safe."

At the abandoned observatory, Vee attached Skye's crystal to her necklace.

"This is incredible. I can feel the energy surging through me!" she said. "I've finally got enough power to catch all the meteors I want. I'll be the greatest scientist in history!"

Back on the aircraft carrier, Skye made up her mind. "If I'm going to get my crystal back, I'm going to need all the power I can get," she said. "I'll have them before anyone knows they are gone!"

Skye found Vee at the observatory.

"I bet those crystals make you feel big and strong. But it doesn't change the fact that you'll always be the smallest pup," said Vee. Then she trapped Skye in a force field and stole the rest of her crystals!

"Time to put all this power to work," Vee said with a giggle.

Vee used her Meteor Magnet and her new superpowers to pull dozens of meteors toward Earth.

"Stop! What you're doing is dangerous," said Skye. "People could get hurt!"

"I tried to do things the right way, but no matter how good I was, I was swept aside and laughed at," replied Vee. "I promised myself I'd never let anyone make me feel small ever again!"

"I know what it's like to feel small. Like, you have to work twice as hard as everyone else just to prove you belong," said Skye. "That's why I risked everything to get my crystal back. But all I did was make things worse."

Just then, Humdinger arrived and reminded Vee of their deal. "One of those crystals is mine," he said.

"Ugh. Fine. A deal's a deal," said Vee.

Humdinger snatched the crystal—and began to grow and grow and grow!

"Ooh, I always knew I'd make it big in Adventure City," he said. "Now if you'll excuse me, I have to pay a visit to the PAW Patrol."

Without their superpowers, the PAW Patrol had to go old-school. The team raced out to face Humdinger.
"Spread out and don't get stepped on," said Ryder.
But before long, Humdinger had them cornered!
"Looks like it's the end of the road, PAW Patrol!" he said.
Thankfully, Nano, Mini, and Tot weren't far away.

"The Junior Patrollers are on a roll!" yelled Mini as he and Tot used a crane to grab onto Humdinger's mustache. The little pups raced up Humdinger's nose—which gave Marshall enough time to snag the crystal out of his jacket pocket!

The Junior Patrollers had saved the day! Without his crystal, Humdinger shrank back down to size and was carted off to jail. After that, the Junior Patrollers helped Zuma free Skye and get the rest of the crystals back from Vee.

Then something amazing happened: Liberty discovered her superpower!

"I'm stretchy! I mean, how did I not think of that?" she said. "I'm a wiener dog. I'm already kind of stretched out in real life!"

When Ryder learned that the meteors were still on their way to Earth, he quickly came up with a plan.

"Skye, I need you to fly up there and destroy as many of those meteors as you can," said Ryder.

"I'll give it everything I've got!" replied Skye.

"If you're going up against those meteors, you'd better take all the power you can get," said Chase, and he and the rest of the PAW Patrol gave Skye their crystals.

"No pup is too small!" shouted Skye as she punched the meteors away. Adventure City was saved!
"Let's hear it for Skye and the Mighty Pups!" cheered the crowd.

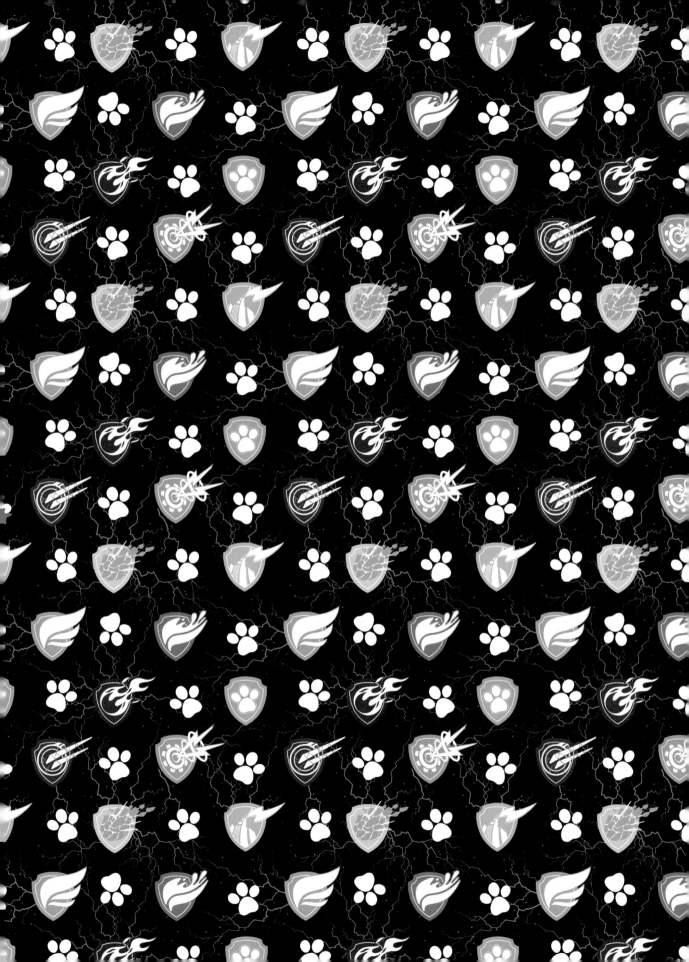

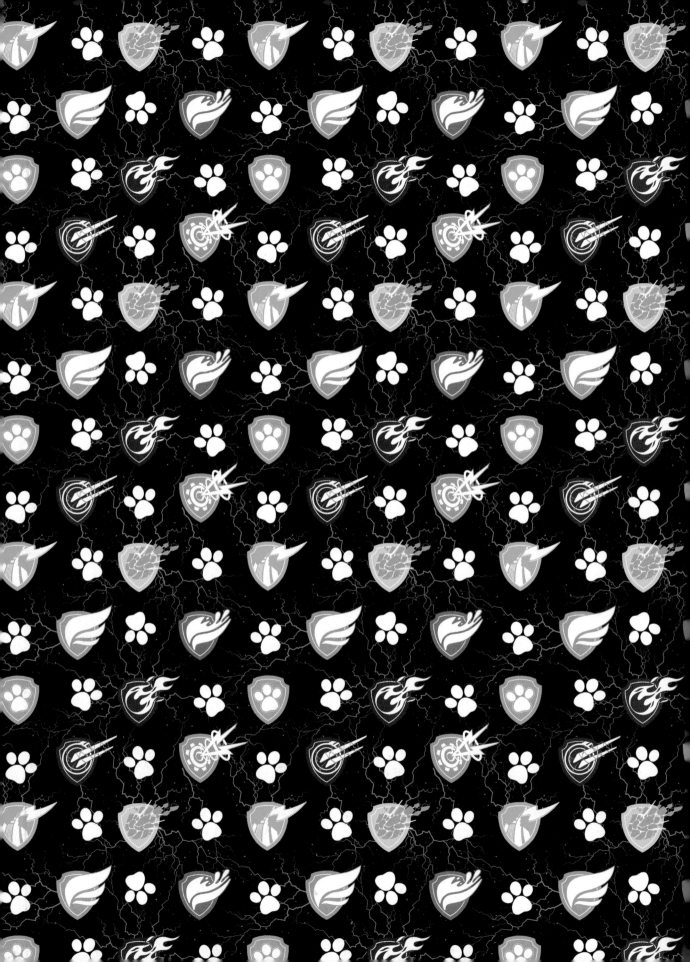